Electrified Skeletons

by

Paul Rogalus

Copyright © 2014
Paul Rogalus

All rights reserved.
The Medulla Review Publishing
retains right to reprint.
Permission to reprint individual
stories must be obtained from author.

Table of Contents

Ronnie and the Stump	4-5
Animal	6-7
Lesarde	8-9
Clarion Call	10-11
The Exploding Man	12-17
The Weird One	18-20
Meet Me at the Met	21-22
The Subterraneans	23-24
Snake Charmer	25
Transformer Man	26-28
Psychos on the Highway	29-31
Border Patrol	32-34
"Flies"	35-36
The Pigeon Wars	37-39
Pain Aids	40-41
Giant Rat	42-43
Life Goes On	44-48
Addicts	49
The GoodTime Bar	50
Test Case	51-52
Johnny Fist	53-54
Acknowledgments	55
Author Bio	56

Ronnie and the Stump

My Uncle Ronnie only had one arm. His left arm was just a stump, about eight inches long—it looked like a delicatessen baloney. He was a big guy—and a very funny guy. Silly funny. He would come up to you and put his arm around your shoulder—buddy-buddy like—only it wasn't an arm—it was an eight inch stump. And when he got into a lively discussion with you, he'd gesture wildly with his stump and jab it into your face. He'd lost most of his left arm in "the big war"—I'm not sure how he *really* lost it—but whenever someone would ask him where he lost his arm, he'd say: "up some German's ass."

I was at my cousin's wedding—and my Uncle Dick was a little bit drunk—when he started talking about Ronnie. Evidently Ronnie had been a really wild and violent guy when he first got back from the war. Very bitter. He had a problem with authority. And back then he had a steel hook attached to the end of his stump. But he got into a lot of drunken bar brawls, and he did a lot of serious damage with the hook, so he had to take it off.

It was when he met my Aunt Angie that he got himself under control. She's even funnier than Ronnie—and tougher too. And Ronnie worshipped Angie—enough to stop cutting people in bars with his hook.

One time I was with Ronnie and Aunt Angie at the town carnival and a local cop was yelling at him for parking illegally. Ronnie got this steely glare in his eyes—and he called the cop a "dirty little maggot." After the cop saw Ronnie's stump, he let him stay parked where he was. Ronnie he winked at me—and then he asked the cop if he could help him find the rest of his arm. The cop said, "How would I do that," and Aunt Angie said, "By crawling up some German's ass." And then Ronnie patted the cop on the shoulder with his stump, and everything was O.K.

Animal

My old roommate, Donnie, used to keep an old chair leg under the driver's seat of his car—it was thick, heavy wood, more like the leg of a sturdy coffee table. He said it was "for emergencies."

I didn't really know Donnie all that well—he'd only been my roommate for one semester my first year at college—and even then he wasn't around a lot. He'd grown up in town, and he stayed at his father's house down by the beach in Narragansett every weekend. And after Christmas he moved back home for good.

I'd come back to Rhode Island that summer weekend to stay with Donnie, hang out at the beach, and drink a lot of beer. We did that. And when Donnie drank—even just a couple beers—he got belligerent. A vicious wild animal.

Donnie was driving late Friday night—fast and reckless—weaving in and out of beach town traffic—and another car—a black Firebird—cut him off at an intersection. Donnie caught up with the Firebird at the next traffic light—he laid on his horn and gave the driver the finger. The driver of the Firebird—another rowdy 20 year-old—gave him the finger back.

"You fucking ass-hole!" Donnie screamed at him. The other driver leaned out of the Firebird and spit—a thick mack at Donnie's windshield. That was it. In a split second, Donnie grabbed his chair leg, hopped out of the car, and completely smashed in the rear windshield of the Firebird in an explosion of broken glass.

A police cruiser was waiting on the opposite side of

the traffic light. It flew over to us, flashers on. Donnie, still holding his chair leg in his hand, screamed out at the cop: "Officer, arrest this man—he spit on my car."

Later on, after Donnie's father bailed him out of jail, Donnie stopped at the counter at the front of the police station and asked the arresting officer if he could have his chair leg back. "Uh, could I have my little toy back," he said, somehow reminding me of Tony Montana in *Scarface*—with his blind arrogance. The cop stared at him, incredulous. "Get the hell out of here," he said.

My old roommate Donnie used to keep an old chair leg under the driver's seat of his car. He said it was "for emergencies." I guess, for Donnie, an "emergency" was any time another wild animal looked him directly in the eye. Or maybe just when someone left the door of his cage open.

Lesarde

In high school, Lesarde had done some pretty weird things. Mainly to get attention. Once he shaved his head completely bald to win a five dollar bet—and he never got paid. Another time he ran around the cafeteria naked—chasing people with an ice cream scoop.

He first name was Laird, but everyone just called him "Lesarde," his last name. He really hated his first name. Every once in a while—like in the middle of a class when we were taking a test—out of nowhere he would just scream out: "I can't believe my parents fucking named me Laird!"

Lesarde had a brother a year younger than him—and HE was actually the *troubled* one in the family. His name was Eulin, but everyone called him "Urine." He had a job cooking at the local Friendly's, but he got fired for doing obscene things to the food.

Even though Laird Lesared was in the same grade as me, he was older than most of my friends, and he had his own car by sophomore year in high school, so people hung out with him—mainly just to get rides. One time he was driving me home from school and he had to stop at his house to pick something up, so I went into his house for just a minute. There were a lot of paintings of naked men on the walls. And in the middle of the living room there was a giant birdcage, the size of a telephone booth—with the door open. Lesarde told me that his father liked to sit inside the cage for hours at a time with the door shut. I just wanted to get the fuck out of there.

I saw Lesarde a few years after graduation—he was working at Burger King. He pretty much looked the same as he had in high school, but on one side of his head his hair was dyed black and the other was bleached blond. And his name tag said: "Larry." I asked him about the name tag. He put his finger to his lips and whispered: "I'm just going by Larry now." And then he got a faraway look in his eyes. His face contorted in anger, and then in a very loud voice he said: "I can't believe my parents fucking named me Laird." But then he calmed right back down again and added: "Oh, do you want fries with that?"

Clarion Call

I.

My friend Jack Maynard always used to like to make the fart in public places—by blowing into the crook of his arm—as loud as he could—and he was really good at it, creating distinctive long, hearty blasts. He'd do it in the school library, and at the supermarket, and sometimes he'd just call people up on the phone and make the fart sound and then hang up.

But his favorite place to fart was at the movies—whenever a scene was too slow or the movie lost his interest. One time a bunch of us were together at the movies in Manchester and the plot got too complex for Maynard, so he made four or five fake fart blasts. And then we heard people in front of us AND people behind us shout out: "Maynard, is that you?"; "Hey, Maynard's here."

II.

It was some anniversary of the death of Elvis Presley, and the East Hartford movie theater was showing and Elvis film festival, starting at midnight—it was supposed to be three Elvis movies and then clips of Elvis in concert. None of us really liked Elvis—except for Donnie—it'd all been his idea in the first place—but we'd been drinking beer most of the night and we just didn't want to go home.

The first movie, *Viva Las Vegas*, was O.K., just kind of lame in places—and so Maynard made the fart sound a few times. When the second movie started, *Kissin' Cousins*—in which Elvis plays two roles—we were bored. But then about halfway through it, something happened, and we just started to laugh. Maybe it was because we were so tired, or maybe it was because the movie was just so stupid—hillbilly Elvis' hillbilly girl cousins seeing city girls in bikini's and saying: "We wanna wear purty underwear too."

Anyway we just laughed non-stop throughout the second half of that movie and all of the third one—almost to the point where I was going to wet my pants.

But when the third movie ended we were wiped. We jumped out into the aisles punch-drunk as soon as the credits started—and we walked up to the exit. All of us except for Maynard, that is. He was still in his seat. And when the house-lights came on in the theater, he started to shout: "Hey, there was supposed to be concert clips!" And then he let out the loudest, angriest blast of a fake fart we'd ever heard.

They sent the theater security guard to get him—but he argued his point about the concert clips until they gave him a free movie pass.

And then we went out for breakfast. Maynard didn't like his eggs, so he made the fart sound—thinking he wouldn't have to pay—but the waitress knew him, and she just slapped him and said, "Shut up, Maynard." And he did.

The Exploding Man

I.

In high school we all took turns driving to the "field parties" on Friday nights—no one really wanted to drive there because you had to drive through acres of corn stalks and broken beer bottles—in order to sit around a big bonfire and drink massive amounts of beer. Once when we were 17 Maynard's car got hit by another car while it was parked at a field party. Actually it was Maynard's father's car—and the rear fender got pretty mangled.

It was a little after one a.m. when we brought the car home—Mr. Maynard, an ex-marine, had been waiting up for us. He came out into the driveway. Maynard started to explain—but his father just put his hand up to shut him up. He crouched down to look at the fender—then he stood up, took a couple of steps toward Maynard, and then punched him as hard as he could—square in the chest. Maynard staggered back a couple of steps, but he didn't fall. He'd been expecting it.

II.

The summer we were 21 Maynard liked to go to this seedy stripper bar called the Rustic Café. One night I went with him, along with our friend Ronnie and this other guy named Lesarde. We had all known Lesarde in high school, and we had all thought that he was an asshole. But Lesarde just had a knack for inviting himself along with us places. He was a wiry, hyperactive guy with oily dark hair. And he never shut up.

Inside the Rustic Café, Maynard walked right to a table near the stage where the strippers danced—a table where a crusty old guy named Johnny was sitting. We had met Johnny at the Rustic the summer before. Johnny had a wooden leg, and he entertained the bar crowd by playing the spoons along with the juke box music as the strippers danced. The dancers all seemed to like Johnny—they let him pick out most of the songs.

Lesarde didn't like the Rustic—he said it was too much of a dive. He sat alone at a table near the door. Maynard called him over, but he just shook his head, stayed at his own table and sulked. Maynard said, "Fuck'im then," and he ordered a picher of Bud.

Johnny had his wooden leg propped up on a chair, and he was wailing with his spoons to an old Allman Brothers song. When the song ended, the local toughs in the bar cheered and hooted—more for Johnny than the dancer. Maynard poured him a beer.

"Where ya' been, Johnny?" Maynard asked him.

"Ain't seen you around for a while."

"I usually come in in the afternoons now. To get away from my wife."

"Afternoons?" Maynard said. "Don'cha work?"

"Nah. I'm retired now."

"What's that, Johnny?" Maynard bellowed out, "you're *retarded*?"

"Nooo," Johnny chuckled. "I'm *retired*."

"You don't look retarded, Johnny." Johnny howled

13

and slapped Maynard on the back. Then he bought us shots of Jack Daniels.

Later on, wooden Johnny was trying to teach Maynard how to play the spoons, but Maynard couldn't get the hang of it—he kept dropping them.

"Forget it, Wild Man," Johnny said to him finally, "you're too stupit."

"Stupid?" Maynard snapped back. "*You're* the one who's retarded, Johnny."

"Nooo," Johnny laughed, slapping his wooden thigh.

An older man in a suit coat approached the stage waving a dollar bill—he tucked it into the dancer's garter belt, and she swooped down and kissed him. Moments later a penny clanked onto the stage floor. Then another penny hit the dancer on the chest.

"Hey, who the fuck's throwin' pennies?" she shouted out, looking in Lesarde's direction. No one said anything. "Well, just cut that shit out," she said. Then slowly she started dancing again.

A moment later, Lesarde stood up and threw a handful of change at the dancer as hard as he could, pelting her face and body.

"You filthy whore," he called out to her.

By the time we got over to Lesarde, Evie the biker barmaid was already pushing him toward the door.

"Fuck you, you pig," Lesarde hissed at her.

Marnard grabbed Lesarde by the sleeve of his plastic-looking leather jacket and tugged him out the door like an unruly dog, saying, "You stupid fucking asshole."

In the back seat of Maynard's car, Lesarde noticed that the sleeve of his leather jacket was torn, and he told Maynard that he was going to have to pay to have it fixed. Maynard just told him to "shut the fuck up," and then for a while Lesarde just sat in the backseat seething, breathing loudly through his nose. And then he started to mutter: first about the ripped jacket, then about the "fuckin' pig dancer," and then about the "fuckin' old loser with the wooden leg." Maynard told him to shut up again, and Lesarde sensed that Johnny was a touchy subject, so that's what he focused on.

"Fuckin' drunken old bum, suckerin you guys into buyin' him drinks."

"We buy *each other* drinks," Maynard snapped at him.

"He bought us shots—he's a good guy."

"He's a drunken fuckin' loser," Lesarde hissed back.

All of a sudden Lesarde lurched forward and grabbed Maynard around the throat, digging his fingernails deep into Maynard's Adam's apple. The car swerved wildly, but Maynard brought it to a skidding stop at the edge of someone's lawn.

Maynard exploded, spinning around gasping for breath, Lesarde's hands still latched onto his throat. He grabbed Lesard by the head and jerked him into the front seat—then he threw the door open and pulled Lesarde outside, heaving him into the middle of the lawn in a pile. I heard a few thumping punches—and in the darkness I could only make out their silhouettes—the primordial man holding his enemy's head in one hand, pounding it into the ground like a big stone—harder, and harder. Ronnie and I rushed over and pulled Maynard away. He spit on Lesarde.

"Asshole," he shouted. "Stupid fucking asshole—big deal about your piece of crap fake leather jacket—big deal! Here!" He tugged off his own denim jacket and violently tore off one of the sleeves and threw it at Lesarde. Then he just stood over

Lesard, snorting like a wild beast. He kicked him in the stomach, and then he was done—I could tell by his eyes.

"Put him in the fucking car," he said to Ronnie.

"Before I kill him."

We drove in silence to Lesarde's house. Ronnie helped him to his door. Maynard shuddered and shook his head, as if he had just taken a shower and his hair was wet. Then he pulled out of Lesarde's driveway.

"Why don't we go back to the Rustic," he said. "I want to buy Johnny and the dancer a few shots."

III.

Another summer visit home—and now 24 year old Maynard is an actual member of the local Elks club—just like his dad. Maynard's father is now retired—hanging out at the Elks club every weekend night. Maynard takes me and Ronnie there one Friday night—to drink and play pool. By 9:30 his father is already sloppy drunk, slurring words and telling endless war stories. Maynard screams at him to shut up—he leads him out into the parking lot—and then he punches him —as hard as he can—square in the jaw. Mr. Maynard falls back against a car—but he doesn't fall. He'd been expecting it. We all had.

The Weird One

My roommate Gerard was a shy, moody, really homely guy—he was an artist. He was 21, but he looked a lot older. He had a small, melon-shaped head, a dark, close-cropped beard which covered most of his face and neck like a fungus, and he was going bald on top. He wore thick, round eyeglasses which made his eyes look enormous. My other roommate Jeff called him "the human fly"; I usually just referred to him as "the weird one"—when he wasn't around.

My hippie friend Molly was really drunk when she first met Gerard in a local bar. I said, "Molly, this is my roommate Gerard."

"Your roommate," Molly blurted out, "so this must be the Human Fly—the one you call "the weird one."

Gerard was crushed. I panicked and tried to lie. "No Molly, you drunken thug, you're getting things mixed up. *I'm* the human fly. *The Fly* is one of my favorite movies—you know—'Help me! Heeeeeeelllp meeeeeeee!" (doing my best human fly imitation).

Gerard didn't buy it. His face was red; his enormous eyes were locked into mine. "The weird one?" he asked me quietly. I just shrugged; there was no way out. Gerard moved off to a table by himself in the back of the bar and started throwing down shots of tequila. After a while, Jeff and I went back and sat with him.

Gerard's face tightened. "Am I really *the weird one*, Paul," he asked.

"Well, yeah, you really are pretty weird, when you get

down to it. So what? So am I. So is Jeff. Jeff is exceptionally weird. What's the big deal."

"Then why am I *the weird one*, and not you or Jeff?"

"Jesus, I don't know, Gerard. That's just the way Molly put it. Forget it, all right?"

Still staring deep into me, Gerard slowly, deliberately picked up two empty beer bottles and dropped his hands beneath the table. He curled his mouth into a sinister smile. Then there was an explosion of glass underneath the table. Gerard raised his fists and put them onto the table, each one tightly squeezing a triangular shard of brown glass and trickling blots of blood onto the table.

"Hey, what the hell happened over there?" the bartender called.

I just stammered like an idiot, "He, uh . . . he's, um . . ."

"He dropped a bottle," Jeff said matter-of-factly.

The bartender said, "Oh, O.K.," and he brought us a towel. We hustled Gerard home.

A few days later I went into Gerard's room to get a book I'd lent him. The room was gross. Partially filled moldy ceramic coffee cups, shabby sweaters of various shades of brown, crumpled up Kleenex, partially painted canvases, and large, torn-up sketch pads. The charcoal sketch on top of the pile caught my eye. It was a dark, smudged sketch of the crucifixion—from an overhead perspective. The body was thin and scrawny; the face was gaunt and homely, with a close-cropped beard, a bald spot, and thick, round eyeglasses. Evidently Jesus had looked exactly like my roommate Gerard, "the Weird One." I got out of Gerard's roommate quick—because I just figured that somewhere in that shabby pile of sketches was a drawing of Satan that looked something like me.

Meet Me at the Met

There used to be an old dive blues bar in Providence called the Met Café—a bunch of my writer friends would go there to drink Guinness stout and write group table poems. There was a very old Black man who was always there, dancing by himself, or sometimes he would conduct the band like an orchestra leader. His name was Frederick Watson Turner—supposedly he had once danced in a movie with Shirley Temple, a very long time ago. He used to just move up to someone in the bar and stare them in the eye for a long time. Sometimes he wouldn't say anything at all, just nod; but sometimes he would stare at someone and then say: "You're an asshole," in a low hiss, and then he'd dance away. As far as I could tell, he was always right. I used to buy him drinks, to stay on his good list; he liked bourbon on the rocks.

And there was usually a pretty rough-looking motorcycle gang at the Met, hanging out around the door, just acting mean. One night I came in wearing a red t-shirt with a picture of Leo Tolstoy on it, and one of the bikers stopped me. He thought it was a picture of "that I-ranian I-uh-tolah guy" on my shirt, and he said that he ought to kick the crap out of me just for being un-American. I told him that it wasn't the ayatollah, that it was Leo Tolstoy, the Russian novelist.

"Russian!" the biker screamed. "That's even worse. That makes you a Communist."

I tried to explain to him that Tolstoy had, in fact, written *before* the Bolshevik revolution, and that Russia hadn't become communist yet, but he didn't seem interested in that. He grabbed me by the shirt collar and twisted it in his fist.

   That's when Frederick came over. Frederick Watson Turner—sort of slid in between the biker and me, moving to the music of the blues band, shaking his head and waggling his finger at the biker. The biker broke his hold on me. Frederick pointed his bony finger at the biker's face and hissed: "asshole." The biker looked down at the floor, deflated, like a guilty child, like the Wicked Witch of the West at the end *The Wizard of Oz*. And then, Frederick patted the biker on the shoulder, and everything was O.K. again. Frederick moved back off to dance in front of the stage again, and I moved off to buy him a bourbon on the rocks.

   I had to pay my dues.

The Subterraneans

It seemed like at least half of my friends at college were stoner-hippie-Dead Heads—but I also had a lot of punk rocker friends—I just didn't party much with them at night—so I didn't really see them in their punk element. But then Iggy and Steve—our closest friends that were serious punks—invited us to a big party at their house.

I went to the party with my hippie roommates Jack and Cubby—and early on in the evening everything was fine. It seemed like a regular party. It wasn't that crowded yet—and they were playing music that we were pretty familiar with—the Talking Heads, Elvis Costello—we felt safe with it. Yeah, we were the only people there not dressed entirely in black, but we were having fun—mingling with punks.

But then something happened. It seemed to get a lot more crowded—with scarier looking punks. And most of the lights went out, and then somebody put on a Ramones album—and <u>cranked</u> it. And all of a sudden it was like the punks became possessed.

They went nuts—lurching and jumping and moshing—slam dancing—smashing violently into each other—into <u>us</u>—all to blaring Ramones machine-gun music:

"Lobotomy! Lobotomy!" The walls started to close in on me. And by the time they put on the Sex Pistols album, I was stumbling around frantically looking for Jack and Cubby. I needed air.

Outside, I found Cubby sitting in a field behind the house, freaking out. He was shaking. "I can't go back in there, Paulie," he said. "There's evil in there."

Eventually Steve came out looking for us. He helped settle Cubby down—with some very soothing Lebanese hash. And then he got Cubby to go back inside the house—partly by promising him that he'd play some Neil Young music.

And by the end of the night, Cubby had gotten most of the punks involved in burning a zorch with him. Cubby loved making zorches. He'd twist a couple of plastic garbage bags together, tie knots in them, and then hang it from the ceiling and set the bottom of it on fire—and have the burning, melting plastic stutter-drip down into a bucket of water. It looked like a special effect from *Star Wars*. The punks watched the zorch, fascinated, completely zoned out—staring in amazement as the melted plastic formed a little floating, burning island of melted glop in the bucket.

Steve put on a Patti Smith album and asked us to "give it a chance." "Hey, it's a lot better than disco," he said. And he was right. The melted plastic island got us thinking about how much we all hated disco. We had a common bond. And Patti Smith sounded pretty good—doing her beat-like poetry rants. And everything was O.K. after that. The party got a lot better.

Snake Charmer

Ben's house—on the muddy brown pond in Rhode Island—Ben and Steve are stoned—and Ben takes off his shirt and stomps into the pond in just his jeans, screaming out that he's going to catch a fish—"just like a bear"—with his bare hands. He splashes around a while, grabbing into the water like a primordial beast—"He *is* like a bear," Steve says. Ben gets frustrated and dives under the water—he's under for a while. When he comes back up—with another primordial shriek—he's holding a black snake in his fist. "I hypnotized it with my left hand," he says, showing us—pulsing his fingers open-closed, open-closed—"and then I caught it with my right hand."

"What're you going to do with it?" Steve asks.

"I don't know," Ben answers. "Wanta eat it?"

"No," Steve says, in his mellow monotone. "No thanks, I'm good . . . besides, snakes are evil."

Ben laughs. "Then we'll give it a joy ride," he says. "Snakes must wanta know how it feels to fly—we all do." And he spins around in circles a few times, holding the snake out at arm's length—and then he lets it go—and it flies—in a high, graceful arc, and then it disappears into the water with a soft plunk.

"Wow," Steve says to me. "That's the most beautiful thing I've ever seen happen to a snake."

Transformer Man

My friend Steve used to look at people and see them with animal faces—usually apes—but sometimes pigs or dogs or bugs of some sort. I thought that was odd at first—that maybe it had something to do with Steve being stoned so much of the time. But now, I just don't know.

One time I was having lunch with Steve at the El Phoenix on Comm. Ave., and I asked him about his animal visions. He gestured to the waiter, a stumpy guy who had a thick, dark uni-brow and a sharply protruding ape-like jaw. "Look," Steve said, "he's still in the process of transforming." The waiter grunted at us and hopped away clumsily.

I could sort of see what he meant.

"And look over there—look at that guy," Steve said, pointing. There was a "man" at the table to our right, eating some sort of casserole plate—or perhaps it was shepherd's pie. Anyway, the man had his face lowered over the plate and he was hoovering up mashed potatoes and corn and ground beef ravenously— without the benefit of using utensils. When he finally raised his face from the plate, it was covered with potatoes and brown gravy.

"I know he's got a lot of slop on his face," Steve said, but if you look closely just above the guy's mouth you can detect the beginnings of a large pig-snout. Oh, he's a pig all right."

As if on cue the pig man snorted, and then mashed his

face back into his casserole plate. Steve shook his head. "He ought to eat out of a trough," he said.

"Yeah, I sort of see it," I said. "So, is it usually apes and pigs that you see people turn into?"

"Well, yeah, a lot of apes," Steve said, "but it's more varied than that." He looked around the restaurant for an example. Off in a dark corner, a couple in their early 20's sat, very seriously kissing each other. Both wore dark, polyester clothing and a lot of jewelry, and both had very dark hair that appeared to be wet. Their kissing became more involved—more intense—their wet faces became plastered to each other—two large, oozing slugs sealing into each other. "There, over there, see them, that 'couple' over there—what do *they* look like to you?"

"Slugs?" I said.

"Yes," he said. "Exactly. They make me sick."

Later on we were walking across the common, and it started to hit me. Steve was on to something. He was just more observant than most people.

A teen-aged couple playfully pranced by us. They were down on all fours on the grass, hopping about each other like excited dogs—taking turns sniffing each others' butts.

"Dog people," I said, pointing. Steve nodded.

"Some days I worry that I might forget what it's like to be human," he said, watching the puppy couple. And then he sighed. "But even so," he went on, "it's still way better than when I see people turning into machines."

He stopped and shook his head.

Wow, I thought, Steve sees machine heads. ***That's* when *I* started worry.**

Psychos on the Highway

At the last minute Cal had decided that he was going to hitchhike out to Montana with me, and I was glad to have the company. For one thing, Cal had some creative strategies for hitching. For instance, I'd hold out my thumb, and Cal would do this crude sort of tap dance to get the attention of the people driving by. And also, with Cal around, it'd be a little less likely that some backwoods country fuck psycho would bludgeon me to death on the roadside—like Jack Nicholson in "Easy Rider." That's also why I got myself a cowboy hat for the trip. To avoid bludgeonings.

And we *did* run into some backwoods country fuck psychos—right away.

We'd spent our first road night in eastern Pennsylvania—it'd just gotten too dark to hitch anymore the night before, so we rolled out our sleeping bags and slept in the tall grass next to the highway. But right at the break of dawn, Cal woke me up. He was scared shitless. He said that there was somebody watching us. He pointed down to a highway pass—to somebody sitting on a bike or a motorcycle.

"That guy's a psycho," Cal said. "He just keeps watching us."

"Yeah, so?" I said. "You're watching him."

"Yeah, but look at him. He's got a giant head. He looks like a sea urchin. And before, just a few minutes ago, he was walking around in circles, very small circles, just walking around and around, kind of jerking his head back and forth, like a horse. Look, there, he's doing it again. Oh, he's a psycho all right."

Cal was right. This guy *was* walking around in circles jerking his head like a horse, like a mad dog—like a . . . psycho. Then he started going faster; he was galloping.

"Holy shit," I said. "He *is* a psycho."

"Yeah. That's what I was saying. We gotta get out of here."

"We can't get out of here, Cal. We don't have a car, remember?"

"Yeah, I know, but still, let's get the fuck out of here."

"Yeah? How? It's kind of hard to flee the scene—hitchhiking."

So we decided to start walking. It was 5 a.m., and there weren't many cars around, but we didn't want to be extras in the road show of *Deliverance*, so we just grabbed our stuff and walked along the highway, away from the psycho with the giant head.

Well, we escaped. Sort of. I mean, we got picked up pretty quickly for five a.m. on a weekday. But we got picked up by another psycho. A different sort of psycho—but a psycho nonetheless. This guy in a big-ass Oldsmobile picked us up—he was in his late fifties or so, and he had this really weird organ music playing on his tape deck. Freaky music. Somewhere between funeral parlor music and carnival music. And it was loud. And he sort of half-turned around to us, and in a spacey, Vincent Price type voice he said, "I'm a BUG on organs."

"What's that?"

"I say, I'm a BUG on organs."

"Oh," I said, "do you play the organ?"

"Oh, no," he said with this twisted smile. I'm just a BUG on organs."

Cal just kind of shrugged his shoulders in defeat, turned to me and said in a really loud voice: "Oh good, another psycho." And then he turned to the driver and said:

"*Are* you a psycho? Are you going to EAT us? Do you stuff dead birds—like Anthony Perkins in the movie *Psycho*?"

Well, the organ guy seemed to get offended by Cal's questions. He cut the ride short, dumping us off just outside of Scranton, saying he was late for work. But that was O.K. with us. We were ready to try for a better ride. We figured the odds were against our running into *another* psycho—at least not for a few hours.

Yeah, it was good to have Cal along for the trip. For protection.

Border Patrol

Somewhere on I ninety in eastern Minnesota Cal and I got picked up by a couple of good ole boys in a jeep, with a cooler full of beer. Heileman's Special Export. They were driving all the way to South Dakota just to buy fireworks. Getting drunk along the way. The driver had on an old baseball cap that said: "Fuck Iran." And he was really proud of it.

And so we drank a lot of Heileman's Special Export beer, and every once in a while one of the guys up front would just go—Yeeeeeeeeeeee—haah! And every once in a while, the driver, Paul, would yell out—PISS—CALL! And he'd pull over to the breakdown lane, get out of the jeep, climb up on the hood, and piss—long distance . . . usually calling out some clever expression, like—"Niagara Falls! . . . Yeeeeeeeeeee—haah!"

And so it was early evening by the time the Minnesota rednecks dumped us off, drunk out of our minds, on the side of route ninety, just over the South Dakota border. They headed off in their Fuck-Iran hats to buy the South Dakota fireworks that they had so coveted. And there we were, stuck on the roadside, too wasted to budge our duffel bags, too wasted to even bother sticking out our thumbs. Too wasted to do anything but fight with each other. Drunk—and after five days living on the road together, we were definitely in the mood to fight. And I knew just the right thing to say to make Cal really mad. I called him a phony intellectual snob. And from there it didn't take us long to just start shouting "fuck you" at each other at the tops of our lungs.

And that's when a big old Plymouth Fury pulled over, right in front of us. And we hadn't had our thumbs out or anything. The car just pulled over, then backed up and stopped right beside us. A drunken middle aged woman rolled down the window and asked us if we-all were wantin' a ride. Her hair looked like it was covered in black shoe polish. The same look as her caked-on eye make-up, that looked like she'd put it on with a trowel. We didn't say anything. We just threw our duffel bags into the back seat and climbed in beside them. They were drinking some kind of clear, strong-smelling alcohol out of peanut butter jars. They asked us questions, but we ignored them for the most part. We were still too busy fighting.

They asked us if we wanted a drink, and the one riding shotgun dangled her bare foot over the car seat, trying to be sexy, I guess. But Cal just looked at it and started to laugh. It was a pretty funny sight. It was a long, hairy foot with deep red nail polish. And once Cal started laughing, I couldn't help but laugh too. And then we couldn't stop. And the ladies, well they got real pissed. They pulled the car over and called us "Yankee faggots" and told us to get the fuck outa their car.

So, we hopped out, and just sorta fell on the ground laughing out of control. And we laughed and rolled around for a long time. Until we felt it start to rain. The rain felt good, refreshing. For about twenty minutes. And then it got annoying. We walked a half mile or so, to a highway rest area with cement picnic tables with individual roofs over them. Cal and I each claimed a table, and lay down on it, and passed out.

I woke up with an aching back and a piercing hangover headache. But then I looked up, and saw the sun just starting to break over the mountains—and it just took the wind out of me—it was so fucking beautiful. I had to wake Cal. And e stared at the rising sun in dumb reverence for a good half-hour, awestruck. It was so amazing that we forgot that we hated each other's guts. And we figured out why we were hitchhiking across the country in the first place.

"Flies"

The summer we lived in Missoula, Montana, Cal and I smoked a lot of pot. We both had jobs at bars, working a few nights a week—and we had a really cheap place to live—so we bought a shoebox full of Montana homegrown and smoked three or four joints a day.

Cal started saving our roaches—and half-smoked joint-buts—first in a coffee cup—but then in a white business-size envelope; he printed the word "roaches" on it—and left it on our coffee table.

We always had a lot of flies in our apartment that summer, so I got a wooden ruler and a big rubber band, and I started hunting flies. I had a lot of free time on my hands that summer—so I did a <u>lot</u> of fly hunting. Seeing Cal's "roach" envelope, I decided to start a collection of my own. I got another white business envelope and printed the word "flies" on it. By the end of the summer, when we were leaving Montana, there must have been 60 or 70 flies in the envelope.

On the day we had to move out of our apartment, I just couldn't bring myself to throw the flies away—and I thought of my friend Steve back in Providence. Steve was the lead singer in a punk rock band called Living with the Bomb, and he was a little twisted, so I thought that he'd appreciate the flies. I took the envelope full of flies—as it was—and sealed it, and on the front of the envelope where it was labeled, I wrote: "flies" c/o Steve Sutton, 15 Wiggins St., Providence, RI 02909. I put an extra stamp on it, and I mailed it.

Two weeks later, while I was still on the road, a 6"x9" manila envelope arrived through the mail at my parents' house in Connecticut. On the front of the envelope it read: "Dead Snake" c/o Paul Lucas, 15 Warren Ave., Rockville, CT.

That's the last time my mother ever opened up my mail.

The Pigeon Wars

Day I.

The Central Connecticut Co-Op Feed Mill factory—in Manchester, CT—the worst job I've ever had. Mind numbing work—amidst mind-numbing machines—loading animal feed into trucks, shoveling corn and chemicals, cleaning storage bins and silos. Machine head syndrome. My co-workers—sideshow freaks—they limp about with molasses-like ooze running down from their nostrils, like Hitler moustaches from breathing in the bonding chemicals that fill the air here. They laugh at me because I'm the only one here who wears the surgical masks they make available to save our lungs. The walking dead.

I get stoned with Donnie, one of the younger truck drivers, during the morning coffee break. And then, since there's no boxcar to unload, I am sent to Warehouse #4 to clean chemical dust, because the dust and grain keeps jamming the conveyer belt gears there.

Warehouse #4—a cold, tin hut—home to a vicious gang of evil pigeons. Mean pigeons—they line up and glare at me from the top of the machine. It's their building. Their eyes follow me everywhere, as I try to clean—but they're freaking me out. I get out of there as fast as I can.

Day II.

It's back to Warehouse #2 again, first thing in the morning—but this time I'm psychologically prepared for the psycho-pigeons. They're there, waiting for me, the evil horde—glaring at me—leering. On an impulse,

I pick up a piece of heavy copper pipe and hurl it—with all my might—at the middle of the pigeon row—dead on—I hit one. The others scatter in chaos. Small victory.

Day III.

There seem to be more pigeons than usual in Warehouse #4 today. A lot more. And they're bigger—with seemingly more human characteristics. There is a definite leader among the pigeons—a massive bird—that looks like Anthony Hopkins in his Hannibal Lectur movies. Another pigeon clearly looks just like Christopher Walken.

They all watch me—intensely—they shriek at me. Their shrieks are taunts—beyond warnings—they're not telling me to get out—they're telling me it's too late—that I've already gone too far. I am a condemned man. They're a ruthless, bloodthirsty gang.

They swoop—dive-bombing me—closer and closer to my head. I cower in a corner—occasionally swatting at them feebly with my broom. When there's an opening, I make a run for it—slamming the warehouse door behind me—and I run for safety in the bathroom in the mill—until I stop shuddering. The pigeons have won.

Day IV.

Ashamed of myself for my cowardice—the next morning, I wake up mean. I look in the mirror feeling like Pink in the movie *The Wall*. No shaving, no washing, no breakfast. No rational thought. I look around for a weapon, and I find part of a Halloween costume I wore a few years ago—a giant chicken head. I have to sneak it in to work in a black plastic garbage bag.

Warehouse #4. Yes, the row of biker pigeons is as big and fierce as ever. Anthony Hopkins is prominent, front and center. Watching me. I turn away from them briefly, like an impressionist getting into character—and I pull on the giant chicken head. With a fearsome burst of energy—all that I have—I spin around and run directly at the pigeons. Many scatter—but Anthony Hopkins stays put, ten feet above me—watching.

I dance, stomping about in front of him—I had intended it to be an aboriginal war dance—but I don't know how to do any aboriginal war dances—so it ends up more like a mosh-pit slam dance—Ramones music fills my head—Beat on the brat with a baseball bat!—Hey-ho—the Blitzkrieg bop—Labotomy! Labotomeee! I lose myself in the dance.

The next thing I know, Donnie is in the warehouse—the boss has sent him to get me to come down for lunch. Donnie is sitting down in the corner by the door—laughing so hard that he is convulsing. But I look up at the pigeons. They are calm. Anthony Hopkins bows to me in respect.

I go down to the main office and give the boss my two weeks notice. There's just no reason to come back.

Pain Aids

I was playing on the Penwood State Park employee softball team with an odd mix of young neo-hippies, crusty farmer types, and a few 20 year-old city punks who were part of some federal employment program. Our official team name was the "Penwood State Park Pileated Woodpeckers," but our uniform T-shirts just said: "Penwood Peckers."

And everyone on the team was number 69.

Just prior to our "big game" against our rival, People's State Forest, our hippie center-fielder Ted brought out a carton of something labeled "Pain Aids." Ted's uncle was a foreman at a textile mill, where they freely distributed Pain Aids to their workers—to get the most work possible out of them. Pain Aids were primarily a mixture of aspirin and caffeine in pill form. Ted gave each player on our team a handful of Pain Aids, claiming that they would make us "wicked fast," and also that we wouldn't get a headache for weeks. So most of us took ten or twelve—even though the carton said that the maximum dosage was four.

But the Pain Aids didn't make us fast at all. We all just stood around feeling wooden and cranky and strung-out. A ball would go by us in the field and we'd just stare at it angrily and refuse to move. I was playing third base, and someone hit a looping popup to me in the first inning, and as I watched it descend it turned into a series of overlapping squares, kind of like a cubist painting by Picasso. It looked like a box kite, but with sharp teeth. I dove out of the way and let it plop to the ground. And the players on the People's State Forest team also started to look very scary to me—like electrified scarecrows with angry faces. They beat us real bad.

So we lost the game by 15 runs, and we were cranky and numb, and none of us could get to sleep at all that night. But none of us got hurt. And we all decided that Pain Aids and softball didn't mix. And so then our second baseman Phil said that he was going to bring a bag of hallucinogenic mushrooms to the next game. We figured it was worth a try.

Giant Rat

There was a giant rat that lived in our basement floor apartment in Boston that year. I lived with two guys that I didn't know very well—and we were all very different personality types. One guy, Tom, worshipped David Bowie. He was a skinny, angular blond guy—with David Bowie hair and clothes. He called himself "Major Tom." The other guy was Irish Mike. Irish Mike liked the Pogues and the Dropkick Murphies, and all things Irish.

The three of us didn't have a lot of common interests to talk about. Therefore, we got stoned a lot, and we'd sit around in the living room—which was also where Irish Mike slept—and zone out, watching TV. And the giant rat would lumber across the living room floor, waddling like an armadillo. And we'd be dazed and numbed out, but we appreciated having the rat to focus on. "Holy crap," someone would say, "that rat is huge!" "It's more like a dog."

The rat would squeeze into a hole behind the radiator in Irish Mike's room and disappear. But then one day the giant rat got stuck. We could hear it—wedged in between the wall and a stud or a pipe in the corner of the living room. It would emit a low squeak and wiggle and push.

We told our landlord about it, but he just sent over an exterminator who left a lot of trays full of poison lying around the apartment. That was the end of the giant rat.

It was sad, like losing a pet. And we didn't talk to each other about it. We just went about our lives, sharing

the painful, tragic glances of parents who silently mourn their lost children.

Life Goes On (The Ballad of Marian and Herb)

Marian was a regular at Antonio's. She came in every day at about 2:30, for free coffee—after the lunch rush had ended. She was a short stump of a woman, with baggy eyes and limp, stringy hair. She always wore the same old red woolen coat, and she always had two or three crumpled grocery bags gripped tightly in her fist. She'd been coming for years. I always gave Marian free coffee—even though she stole one of my tips once. A few people had seen her swipe the tip right off the table—but Marian always denied it, rant-babbling her way out of it: "I didn't take it—it wasn't me—I know who it was, but it wasn't me." "Yeah, who took it then?" "It—wasn't me—I know who it was, but it wasn't me."

She knew the names of all the people who worked in the restaurant—and she knew the names of many of the regular customers. She would usually come in with something to show everyone, something someone had given her—or a photograph someone had taken of her:

"Paul, here, I wanna show you this—it's a pitcher. Don't laugh, O.K.—don't laugh."

"I won't laugh, Marian."

"Here, look." It was always the same pose: her cheeks puffed out like a blowfish, her enormous, baggy saucer eyes bugging out. "It's me!"

"No, is it, Marian? Really? You look very nice."

"Where's Lisa—I wanna show Lisa. Don't laugh."

She'd show Lisa the picture—and then she'd show the

cooks, and the dishwasher—and then the customers.

There was another "regular" at Antonio's that most of us at the restaurant had always associated with Marian—since they were both regulars, and since they were both so strange. He was a small, thin, middle-aged man with the face and hair of a skinny rat. His left eye was always half-closed. He shuffled when he walked, holding his little arms stiffly out in front him like a Tyrannosaurus Rex. His name was Herb. He couldn't speak very well—when he tried to, he made a mixture guttural grunts and a low-pitched wheeze. Herb usually came in earlier in the afternoon than Marian did—and Herb always paid for his coffee. Full price.

"Uhn-uhn, c-coffeereglar," Herb would stammer out in one word. Then he'd hand me a pile of change and make me count out seventy-five cents and give the rest back. Herb also had a difficult time with the sugar. Every day Herb's table would wind up looking like a family of five had eaten at it, without plates—all from one "coffeereglar."

None of us had ever actually seen Marian and Herb together—we just assumed they knew each other. Then one day I saw them actually meet for the first time. They were sitting two tables apart—but they were the only customers in the restaurant.

"Hi," Marian called out loudly to Herb. "What's your name?"

Herb grunted. Marian looked at me. "I never seen him before. What's his name?"

"Don't you know him, Marian?"

"No, I never seen him before." She turned back to Herb. "What's your name?"

Herb grunted a few times before he came out with a wheezy "Uhn, uhn, Herb."

"Hi Herb. Nice ta meet'cha."

Another customer came in, glanced at Marian and Herb, and moved to the far corner of the restaurant. After I brought the customer a menu, Marian called me over.

She whispered to me, giggling: "He said he likes me. Herb. And I never met him before today." Her breath reminded me of old, wet sneakers.

"Good for you, Marian," I said. "Herb's a pretty cool dude."

"He said he likes me." Herb was hunched over his table, looking like a wet rag. "He said he likes me and he wants ta marry me. And I just met him today."

Herb got up and struggled to get his coat on.

"Goodbye Herb!" Marian called as Herb shuffled to the door. "See you tomorrow!" Then she turned to me to explain. "He's going into Boston on the subway. I hope he makes it."

"Why don't you go with him, Marian."

"No," she said. "I'll see him tomorrow. He said he'd buy me lunch tomorrow."

Herb crossed the street and shuffled past the subway

stop and out of sight.

The next day Marian showed up at the restaurant earlier than usual. I was busy with a few tables in the back, and I swung by and gave Marian a free cup of coffee to keep her quiet.

"I'm waitin' for Herb," she called out as I hurried away.

Herb shuffled into the restaurant a few minutes later and sat at the table next to Marian's. I swung by and asked him if he wanted coffee.

"Uhn, uhn, yes, coffeereglar."

By the time I brought Herb his coffee, Marian had moved over to his table and was sitting beside him. Herb gave me a dollar, and I gave him his change, and rushed off to check on my other customers.

From the back of the restaurant I could hear blurts of Herb's excited babble. Herb was still ranting when I got to him—he was hysterical. And Marian was gone. Herb showed me his empty wallet, and he stuttered out the word: "s-s-stolen."

"Marian took your money, Herb? How much—how much did you have?"

Herb just kept grunt-whining "s-s-stolen" and shaking his head. I gave him a few dollars from my tip money, and Herb started to quiet down. As I was picking up the order for my other customers, I saw Herb shuffle out of the restaurant, still shaking his head and mumbling. I never saw him again.

Marian stayed away from Antonio's for almost three

weeks. Her personal record. But then, late one afternoon, just before the shift change, I was sitting at the table in the back of the restaurant counting my tips, and I heard Marian's voice—she was talking to Maggie, the new waitress.

"Hi, my name's Marian," she bellowed out. "What's yours?"

I just smiled and stood up, and I went to go get Marian her free cup of coffee.

Addicts

I was in my early twenty's, working lunches as a waiter at Giorgio's Italian Restaurant just outside of Boston—and I got asked out on a date by a 40 year old recovering cocaine addict with three kids who was on parole for punching another woman. She wanted me to go to a karaoke bar with her. Her youngest son used to come in to get Cokes to go, and he always had to flatten his dollar bills out before he would give them to me—so that they didn't have any wrinkles in them. His mother said that growing up in a crack house will do that to a person.

The GoodTime Bar

The GoodTime Bar—in downtown Lafayette, Indiana—"where every night is Halloween." Stiff Kitten, a heavy metal hair-band cranks out Ratt and Motley Crue covers—to sweaty bikers and local metal-heads—cramped together into this seedy shack. Wiry biker chick in a fight with her boyfriend—lifts him up by his t-shirt and rams the back of his head against the battered wall—making the tables in the back shake—and the skinny, middle-aged drying out ex-drunk bartender looks nervous—too scared to pick up the baseball bat behind the bar. And then the heavy metal hair-band breaks into AC/DC—just to help break up the brawl—just to make everyone happy.

Test Case

Once when I was in grad school, I was a subject in a psychological study, investigating the effects of alcohol upon the mental capacities of young men. I got paid ten dollars an hour—to drink alcohol. The study worked like this: I had to sit at a little desk in a tiny, little box of a room for two hours a clip, and drink vodka and some kind of soda out of a beaker. And then they had me answer questions on a test sheet every twenty minutes—like the tests in school where you fill in little circles. But then they made me put on a set of headphones to listen to music with—while I sat there and drank. The thing was, they kept playing the same tape over and over again—always the same singer. Michael Bolton, over and over. It wasn't <u>so</u> bad the first session—it just gave me a headache. The next night when I went back I thought they'd put in a different tape. But, no. Same old god damn Michael Bolton tape. And it was just lame. Whiny elevator music. So when the guy in the white lab coat came in with my test paper to fill out, I said to him, "Please, can't you change the god damn tape? It's driving me nuts." But he said no, the music had to be the same throughout the experiment for everyone. I <u>guzzled</u> that next beaker of vodka. I had one <u>hell</u> of a headache when I left that second night—and it was more from Michael Bolton than from the vodka—it was good vodka—smooth.

I had to come back two nights later for my third session—and once again, same god damn Michael Bolton tape. Well, I just got mad. I yelled at the guy in the white lab coat, called him all sorts o' names. I said, "You change the music you sadistic bastard. You just take that tape out to the woods and shoot it!" And instead of filling in the little circles on my test sheet, I just wrote about how I'd like to kick Michael Bolton's ass. In great detail. But, eventually, I just got numb to it. I even fell asleep with the headphones on. They woke me up—and sent me home on the commuter rail. I went home and stared at the wall for the rest of the night—LIKE A DUMBASS. Scared the shit out of my girlfriend. She wouldn't let me go back for the last session. "Yeah, you need the money," she said. "But Michael Bolton is stealing your soul."

I still got sixty bucks. And it's funny . . . I still like vodka. Just not Michael Bolton.

Johnny Fist

A muscle-bound young blond man strode up to the bar and slapped both of his palms down hard on the wooden counter to get Sherry's attention. She looked at him, expressionless. He held up six fingers.

"Six beers for Johnny Fist." He was wearing a tight t-shirt that read: Johnny Fist will Kick some Ass tonight.

"The limit is two," Sherry answered flatly, putting down two bottles.

Johnny Fist threw some bills onto the bar and smiled, picking up the beers.

"I'll be back," he announced.

I'd only been working at the bar for a couple weeks. I'd never seen this guy before.

"What's the deal with the inflatable man?" I asked Sherry.

"Johnny Fist? He's here quite a bit. He's a small time professional wrestler—you know, like in that movie with Mickey Rourke. He wrestles down at the armory—I guess he almost always loses. Somebody told me his tights have a black circle on the crotch, with a bright red fist in the center."

"Figures," I said, watching Johnny as he worked his way over to a table of girl-women near the bar.

"Who's got a cigarette for Johnny Fist?" he barked out.

A girl in leather jacket, with a Nascar t-shirt gave him one. Johnny Fist nodded.

"Johnny Fist likes action," he said with a smile.

"Oh Jesus," I said, shaking my head.

"He's all talk," Sherry said. We watched him pose for the girl-women, flexing his muscle. "I carded him the first time he came in." Sherry smiled. "His real name is Wendell."

Acknowledgments

"Lesarde" and "Flies": *Babel Magazine*
"The Exploding Man": *Nerve Cowboy*
"Life Goes On (The Ballad of Marian and Herb)":
Thunder Sandwich
"The Stump": *Flashshot*
"The Weird One": *Centripetal*
"Border Patrol": *The Bukowski Hangover Project*
"Snake Charmer": *Sleet*
"Transformer Man": *WEIRDYEAR*
"Addicts": *100 word story*
"Hunter Thompson's Ashes": *Drunk Monkeys*

Author Bio

Paul Rogalus teaches English at Plymouth State University, in New Hampshire. His full-length play *Crawling From the Wreckage* was produced in New York City in February 2002 by the American Theatre of Actors, and his one act plays have been produced in New York, Chicago, and Boston. His short screenplay, "Sid and Walt," won screenwriting contests at the Wildsound Film Festival in Toronto and at the PictureStart Film Festival in New York City, and his short script, "Trans," won the Woods Hole Film Festival Short Screenplay Award. A chapbook of his micro-stories entitled "Meat Sculptures" was published by Green Bean Press.

Printed in the USA
CPSIA information can be obtained
at www.ICGtesting.com
LVHW040205181124
796853LV00005B/714